T0090428

Order this book online at www.trafford.com
or email orders@trafford.com

Most Trafford titles are also available at major online book retailers.

Printed in Victoria, BC, Canada.

ISBN: 978-1-4269-1803-2 (soft)
ISBN: 978-1-4269-1804-9 (hard)

Library of Congress Control Number: 2009939956

Our mission is to efficiently provide the world's finest, most comprehensive book publishing service, enabling every author to experience success. To find out how to publish your book, your way, and have it available worldwide, visit us online at www.trafford.com

Trafford rev. 10/26/2009

 www.trafford.com

North America & international
toll-free: 1 888 232 4444 (USA & Canada)
phone: 250 383 6864 ♦ fax: 812 355 4082

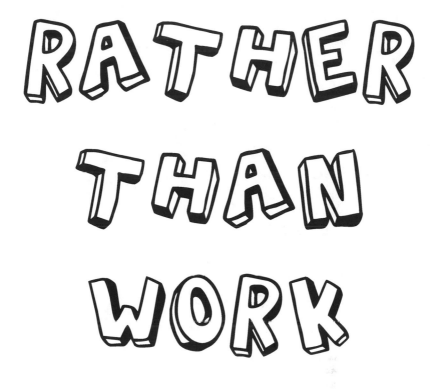

RATHER THAN WORK

Tim Slaven and Geoff Yeagley

1

I would rather be strung up like a piñata and smashed with baseball bats by angry children...than go to work tomorrow.

2

I would rather pick up dog feces with my teeth...than go to work tomorrow.

3

I would rather travel to Maine, jump on a fishing boat, and receive a circumcision by a 13lb lobster... than go to work tomorrow.

4

I would rather clean the Detroit train station's urinals with my tongue...than go to work tomorrow.

5

I would rather be used as the S.W.A.T. team training dummy during sharpshooter practice...than go to work tomorrow.

6 I would rather steal Marty McFly's DeLorean, go back to 1985, and get repeatedly punched in the face by a 19yr old, brass knuckled Mike Tyson...than go to work tomorrow.

I would rather be Michael Vick's new pet toy poodle...than go to work tomorrow.

8

I would rather once again get back in McFly's DeLorean, go back in time to 1985, and receive 9 innings worth of pitches to my face from a 23yr old Roger Clemens... than go to work tomorrow.

I would rather go bungee jumping with a broken rubber band...than go to work tomorrow.

10

I would rather have Tiger Woods attempt to use my testicles in a long drive contest...than go to work tomorrow.

11

I would rather wear a suit made out of chicken and jump into an alligator infested lake...than go to work tomorrow.

12

I would rather eat 3 bowls of thumb tacks, open my mouth wide, and allow Wolverine to reach down my throat with his bladed right hand, slowly pulling them out one by one...than go to work tomorrow.

13

I would rather wrap my entire body in fly paper, roll around in cocaine, and lock myself in a metal room with a blow torch and 33 crack addicts...than go to work tomorrow.

14

I would rather floss my teeth with Bea Arthur's thong...than go to work tomorrow.

I would rather my skull used as a baseball by Alex Rodriguez after a steroid binge...than go to work tomorrow.

16

I would rather be massaged
with bbq sauce by Hannibal Lecter...
than go to work tomorrow.

I would rather hang myself by my pubic hair from the top floor of the Empire State Building...than go to work tomorrow.

18

I would rather receive a reach around from Freddy Krueger...than go to work tomorrow.

19

I would rather do jumping jacks in a puddle, during a large scale thunderstorm, wearing copper underwear...than go to work tomorrow.

20

I would rather have my nose pierced with an ice pick by Sharon Stone...than go to work tomorrow.

21

I would rather go to Chili's and lay my face on a sizzling fajita skillet...than go to work tomorrow.

22

I would rather use my face as a toilet bowl after an all you can eat burrito contest...than go to work tomorrow.

23

I would rather glue my eyelids to an F-18 during takeoff from an aircraft carrier...than go to work tomorrow.

24

I would rather remove my pants, velcro my hands behind my back, be suspended in mid-air, and allow Ultimate Fighter trainees to practice kicking and punching on my nut sack...than go to work tomorrow.

I would rather be driven home by Lindsay Lohan after an all night bender...than go to work tomorrow.

26

I would rather get kicked in the genitals by David Beckham... than go to work tomorrow.

27

I would rather rub SuperGlue on my lips, and make out with the space shuttle as it's seconds away from lift-off, than go to work tomorrow.

28

I would rather have a sumo wrestler put on high heels and tap dance on my face than go to work tomorrow.

29

I would rather blindfold myself, take off all my clothes, and jump around in a bounce house full of rusty hatchets...than go to work tomorrow.

30

I would rather be covered in bird seen and dropped in the middle of a cock fight...than go to work tomorrow.

31

I would rather have root canal performed with a chain saw by Stevie Wonder...than go to work tomorrow.

32

I would rather dress up like a seal, rub myself with dead fish, and go swimming with great white sharks...than go to work tomorrow.

33

I would rather use a cheese grater to remove all my body hair... than go to work tomorrow.

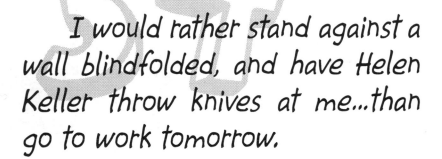

I would rather stand against a wall blindfolded, and have Helen Keller throw knives at me...than go to work tomorrow.

35

I would rather cover myself in chocolate sauce, roll in powdered sugar, and walk through a treatment center for prader-willi syndrome... than go to work tomorrow.

36

I would rather try to catch a window A/C unit dropped from the top floor of the Sears Tower...than go to work tomorrow.

37

I would rather guess the first show's weights of The Biggest Loser contestants by having them stand barefoot on my face...than go to work tomorrow.

38

I would rather use my face as a human dartboard...than go to work tomorrow.

39

I would rather put my testicles in a Slap Chop and smash repeatedly...than go to work tomorrow.

I would rather stand on the 3rd floor ledge of a building, swan dive into a full dumpster outside a Chinese fish market, and remain on the bottom until able to eat my way out...than go to work tomorrow.

I would rather go hunting with Dick Cheney...than go to work tomorrow.

42

I would rather be duct taped to a chair and forced to watch a Sex in the City marathon with a group of man hating women...than go to work tomorrow.

43

I would rather place my tongue in an electrical outlet while standing in a pool of water...than go to work tomorrow.

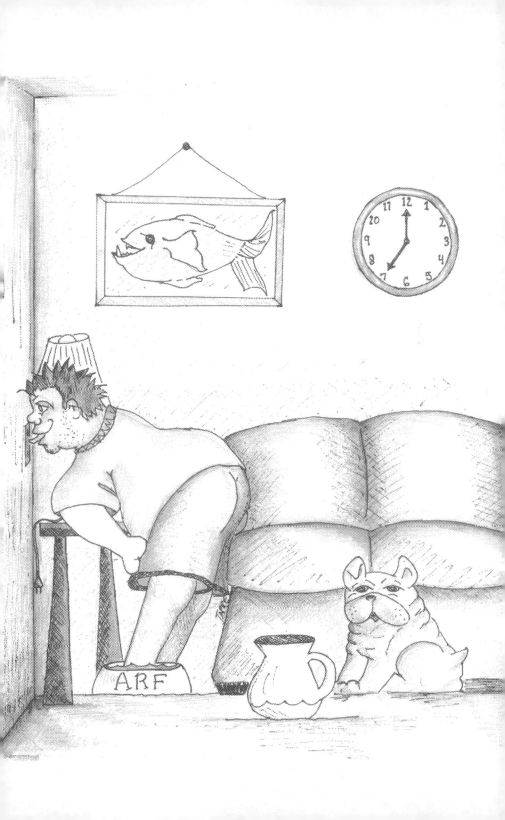

I would rather color in my pupils with liquid paper, and walk a dental floss sized tight rope over a water tank containing 500 sting rays and the Crocodile Hunter... than go to work tomorrow.

45

I would rather prop my mouth open with a piece of wood and entice zoo monkeys to sling their fecal matter in my direction...than go to work tomorrow.

46

I would rather be used as a mating dummy for humpback whales...than go to work tomorrow.

47

I would rather go to Hawaii, rent a helicopter, and swan dive into an active volcano while doused in gasoline...than go to work tomorrow.

I would rather grow more hair on my body than Chewbacca, then have it waxed off one inch at a time...than go to work tomorrow.

49

I would rather sew my ass shut, go to Taco Bell, and eat spicy burrito's until I explode...than go to work tomorrow.

50

I would rather challenge the contestants of the World's Strongest Man Competition to a game of dodgeball using claw hammers... than go to work tomorrow.

51

I would rather drink a bottle of Nyquil and fall asleep on a fire ant mound...than go to work tomorrow.

52

I would rather glue magnets to myself, throw Leonardo Diccaprio overboard, and stick myself to the front of the Titanic in the king of the world pose as an iceberg sets course for my testicles...than go to work tomorrow.

53

I would rather play paddy cake with Edward Scissorhands... than go to work tomorrow.

54

I would rather take Lance Armstrong's spandex immediately following the Tour de France, wring them out into a plastic cup, and sip as if a fine martini...than go to work tomorrow.

55

I would rather give myself a quick dry cement enema...than go to work tomorrow.

56

I would rather be locked in a room with nothing but an electric knife, a freezer, and Jeffrey Dahmer...than go to work tomorrow.

57

I would rather shove magnets up my ass, and casually stroll through a knife shop... than go to work tomorrow.

58

I would rather be Osama Bin Laden's only bodyguard during his guest speaking engagement at a New York City gun show...than go to work tomorrow.

59

I would rather be blindfolded, dropped in the middle of the woods, and be hunted down by Rambo than go back to work tomorrow.

60

I would rather staple Shamwow's all over my body, and roll around the floor of a convention center's men's room after the toilets have backed up during a beer festival, than go to work tomorrow.

61

I would rather receive a friction dance from Andre The Giant...than go to work tomorrow.

62

I would rather have my mouth taped shut, be sewn into a gerbil costume, and locked in a dark closet with a 10 gallon bucket of Vaseline and Richard Gere...than go to work tomorrow.

63

I would rather put on a tin man suit, and test all the electrical outlets in my neighborhood with a fork...than go to work tomorrow.

I would rather transport used adult diapers to the dumpster by my teeth...than go to work tomorrow.

65

I would rather be dressed in a backless hospital gown, and dropped in general population of a maximum security penitentiary during a prison guard strike...than go to work tomorrow.

I would rather have a 500lb woman wearing high heels perform the River Dance on my testicles... than go to work tomorrow.

67

I would rather have my tonsils removed with a pitchfork...than go to work tomorrow.

68

I would rather tie my hands behind my back, walk into a McDonald's kitchen, and bob for apples in a deep fryer...than go to work tomorrow.

69

I would rather climb Mt. Everest with the drummer from Def Leppard...than go to work tomorrow.

70

I would rather go naked to Chuck E Cheese, swallow a roll of tickets, and spit them out one at a time as aggressive children hit me in the privates with a Wac-a-Mole mallet...than go to work tomorrow.

71

I would rather have Richard Simmons liposuction my ass fat with his mouth and a crazy straw... than go to work tomorrow.

72

I would rather have King Kong perform a 45 minute bongo solo on my testicles...than go to work tomorrow.

73

I would rather be on the 400th floor of a burning building, passed out from smoke inhalation, and carried down a ladder to safety by being strapped to the back of Christopher Reeve...than go to work tomorrow.

I would rather be strapped to an electric chair and tea-bagged be every member of The Village People...than go to work tomorrow.

75

I would rather go to an outdoor chili cook-off festival, and empty all the porta-potties with a Dixie cup...than go to work tomorrow.